This Little Tiger book belongs to:

_____

_____

_____

For Charlotte, with my love

~ T C x

For my lovely friend Yvonne, and her mummy

~ A E

LITTLE TIGER PRESS
1 The Coda Centre, 189 Munster Road,
London SW6 6AW
www.littletiger.co.uk

First published in Great Britain 2013
This edition published 2014

A CIP catalogue record for this book is
available from the British Library

Printed in China • LTP/1800/0757/1013

2 4 6 8 10 9 7 5 3

I
Want
My
Mummy!

Tracey Corderoy

Alison Edgson

LITTLE TIGER PRESS
London

Arthur was playing dragons when his mummy came in.

"Look, I'm flying!" Arthur giggled.

"Oh!" smiled Mummy. "What a busy little dragon! Are you ready to go to Granny's house? She's looking after you today, remember?"

"**Raaargh!**" roared Arthur grumpily.
"But I want to stay with YOU!"
He'd never been apart from
Mummy for the whole day before.

"You can show Granny your dragon suit!" said Mummy. "You'll be *just* like her toy dragon, Huffity."

"Huffity!" Arthur cried. "I can play dragons with Huffity! *Let's go!*"

And off they went.

When they got to Granny's house, Granny gave Arthur a big, squashy hug.

"What a splendid little dragon you are!" she said.

"Just like Huffity!" Arthur cried, and he skipped inside to find him.

But all too soon it was
time for Mummy to go.
    Arthur held up his
little nose for a special
Mummy cuddle.
    "Rubby noseies,"
whispered Mummy.
    "Rubby noseies,"
sniffed Arthur.

Then he waved and
waved and waved until
Mummy was gone.

"Shall we do some painting?"
Granny asked, but Arthur just
wanted Mummy.

"**Raaargh!**" he grumped.

"Dragons don't paint!"

"Or we could make dragon music?" smiled Granny, banging on a drum.

"Oh!" said Arthur, edging closer. Dragons *did* like drums.

But then . . .

ding - dong!

went the doorbell.

"**Mummy's back!**" Arthur cried.

But it *wasn't* his mummy . . .
"**Raaargh!**" grumped Arthur.
"Dragons don't want LETTERS!"

"It's all right," Granny said softly. "Mummy will be back later."

Arthur gave a little dragon sniff.

"Look, Arthur!" said Granny. "I've got some *treasure*. But I need a big, brave dragon to guard it."

"Me!" cried Arthur. "I'm big and brave!" He would hide it in a cave.

So he hurried into the garden to find one.

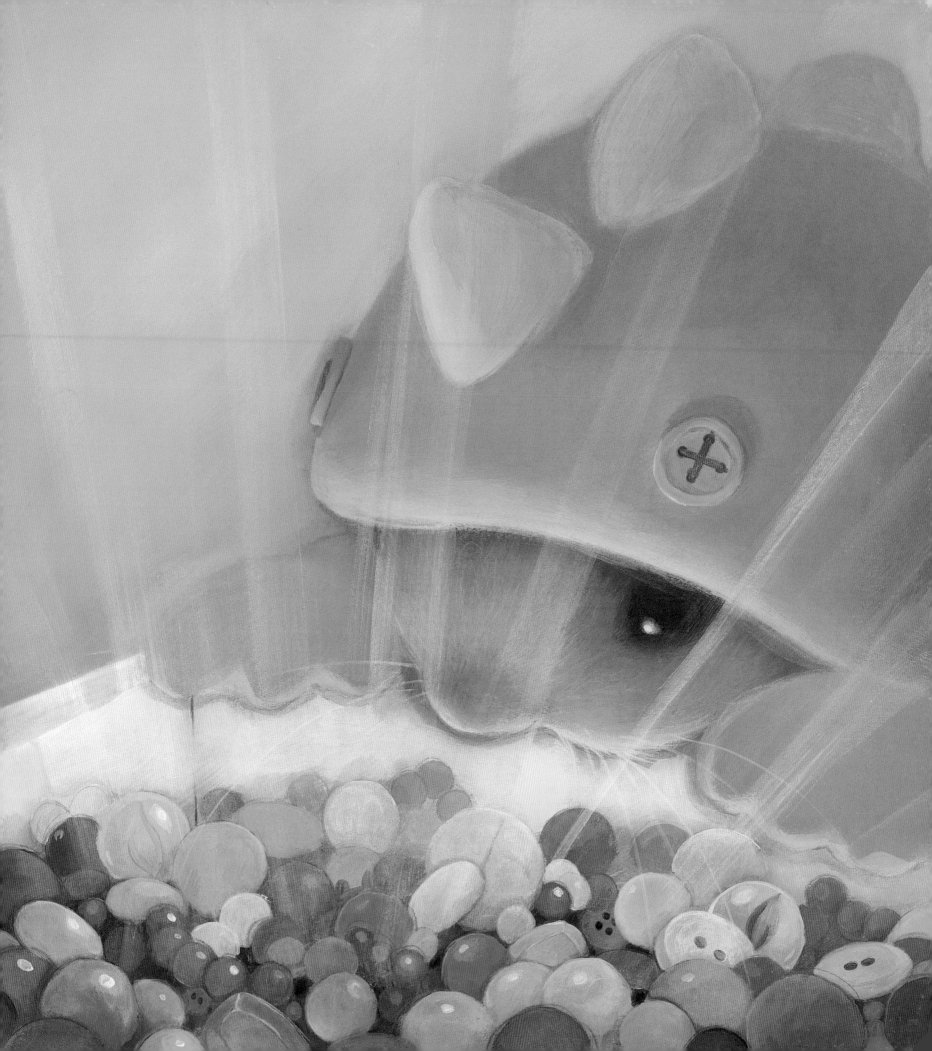

When Arthur had found a fine
dragon cave, he sat in it,
guarding his treasure.
    "Hee hee!" he giggled.
No one would find it here!
    Then suddenly, he
heard another . . .

ding-dong!

"Mummy!" cried Arthur,
racing inside . . .

But it was just Granny's friend, returning an umbrella she had borrowed.

"**Raaargh!**" grumped Arthur. "Dragons don't want UMBRELLAS!"

"Oh dear," Granny sighed. "Why
don't we have some lunch?"
They sat together at the table.

"Mummy will be back very soon," said
Granny, pointing at the clock. "When the
big hand gets to the number twelve and
the little hand gets to the four! But now
I need a costume too! Let me see . . ."

Granny threw a tea towel
around her shoulders.
"Look, I'm a knight!" she cried.
"This is my cloak! And this is
my sword!"
"Wow!" Arthur gasped.
"Now I'm off to find some
treasure!" Granny-Knight
smiled.

"**Raaargh!**" giggled
Arthur-Dragon. "You
won't get mine!"

He raced off to his deep, dark cave to guard his shiny treasure. "Granny-Knight's coming to catch you!" Granny chuckled.

"Hee heeeeee!" squealed Arthur,
as she tickled his tummy.
Then they played knights and
dragons all afternoon, until . . .

ding-dong!

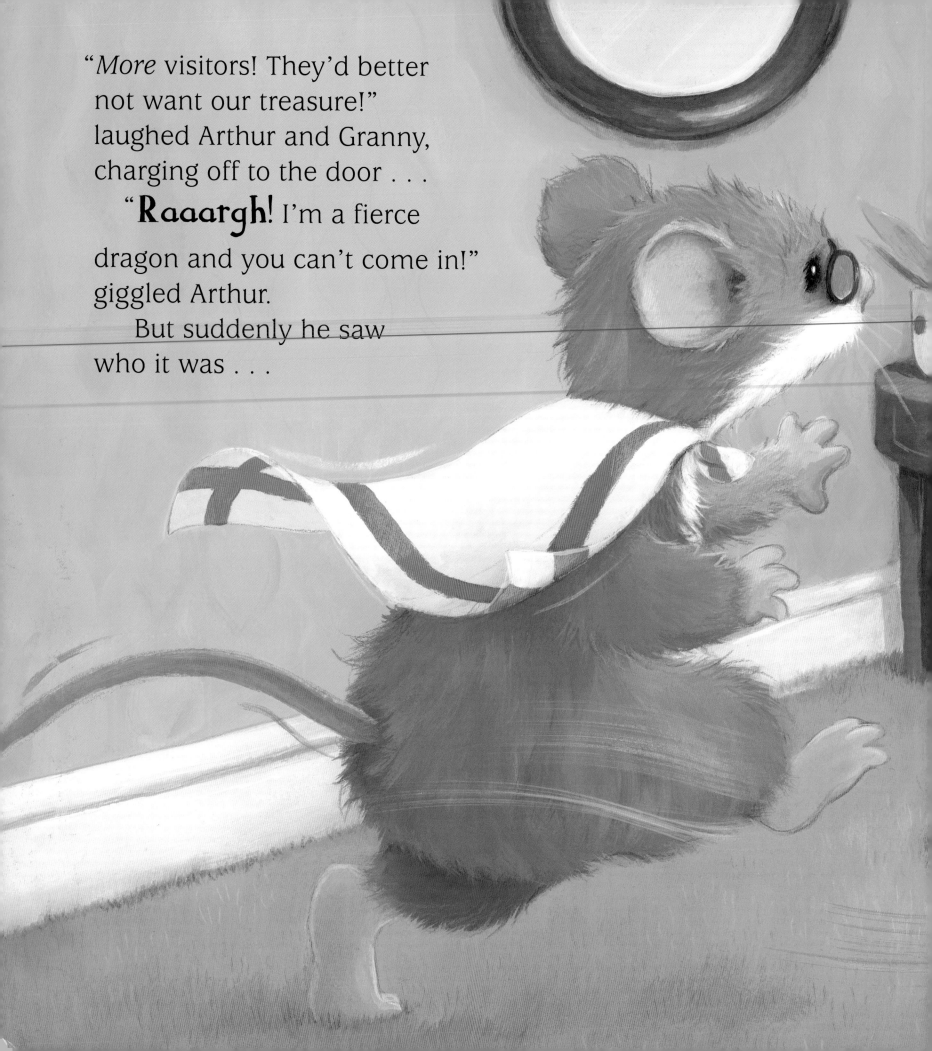

"*More* visitors! They'd better not want our treasure!" laughed Arthur and Granny, charging off to the door . . .

"**Raaargh!** I'm a fierce dragon and you can't come in!" giggled Arthur.

But suddenly he saw who it was . . .

"**Mummy!**"
cried Arthur.
      And Mummy gave
Arthur the biggest
hug ever!

"Have you had fun?" she asked him.
"Lots and lots!" said Arthur. "Dragons
love playing with their grannies
so much . . . But no one gives
cuddles like Mummy!"

More adorable books from

Little Tiger Press!

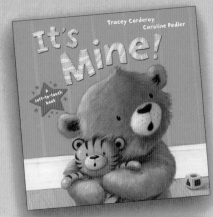

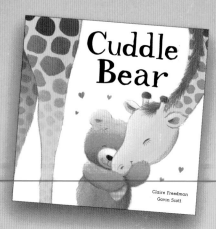

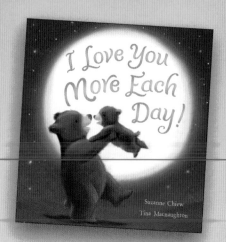

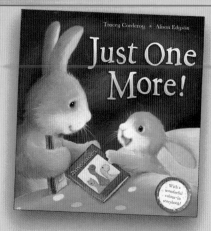

For information regarding any other Little Tiger Press
titles or for our catalogue, please contact us:
Little Tiger Press, 1 The Coda Centre,
189 Munster Road, London SW6 6AW
Tel: 020 7385 6333 • Fax: 020 7385 7333
E-mail: info@littletiger.co.uk • www.littletiger.co.uk